North of Danger
❋ Dale Fife ❋

Map and decorations by Haakon Sæther

A Unicorn Book

E. P. Dutton   New York

Library of Congress Cataloging in Publication Data

Fife, Dale.   North of danger.

SUMMARY: Twelve-year-old Arne undertakes a two-
hundred-mile trip on skis to warn his father of a
German invasion of their town on the Norwegian
archipelago of Svalbard.
1. Svalbard—History—Juvenile fiction.   2. World War,
1939-1945—Norway—Svalbard—Juvenile fiction.
[1. Svalbard—History—Fiction.   2. World War, 1939-
1945—Norway—Svalbard—Fiction]   I. Title.
PZ7.F4793No 1978   [Fic]   77-26199   ISBN: 0-525-36035-2

Published in the United States by E. P. Dutton, a Division
of Sequoia-Elsevier Publishing Company, Inc., New York

Published simultaneously in Canada by Clarke,
Irwin & Company Limited, Toronto and Vancouver

Editor: Emilie McLeod   Designer: Riki Levinson
Printed in the U.S.A.   First Edition
10 9 8 7 6 5 4 3 2 1

To Lorene and Charles Beasley
Midsummer 1974

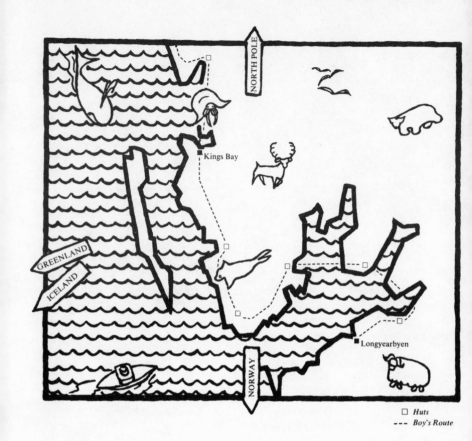

NORTH POLE

Kings Bay

GREENLAND

ICELAND

NORWAY

Longyearbyen

☐ Huts
--- Boy's Route

❃ Foreword ❃

The story of twelve-year-old Arne Kristiansen, in the Archipelago of Svalbard, is a fictionalized account of a true incident.

Svalbard, more often called Spitsbergen, lies within the Arctic Ocean approximately ten degrees, or four hundred nautical miles, from the North Pole. It is under the sovereignty of Norway.

In August of 1940, British warships stood in Advent Bay off Longyearbyen, the capital. Their mission was to evacuate the entire population, some three thousand people, most of them coal miners and their families.

The German Army, which had already taken over Norway, was expected to invade Spitsbergen to cut off the shipment of polar coal to Europe and to destroy or take over weather and radio stations critically necessary for the safety of Allied shipping.

Unknown to the authorities, one person, Arne Kristiansen, was left behind. This is the story of what happened after the ships moved out of the harbor and the long dark polar winter was about to close down.

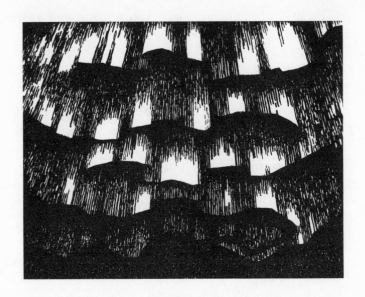

❄ 1 ❄

Arne was the first to see the rescue ships creep into Longyearbyen Harbor under cover of early morning fog.

A battleship, two destroyers.

Apprehension jolted him down to his toes. Not the evacuation. Not yet. Not until his father returned.

He pushed away from the breakfast table so violently his chair banged against the cupboard, rattling the dishes. He sprang to the window.

The Paulsons—mother, father, Nils—with whom he had lived for the weeks his father was away, crowded behind him.

"The British!" Nils, who was Arne's friend and almost his age, shouted. "The British. They're here."

"Thank God," Fru Paulson said. "We're safe now. They'll evacuate us before the Nazis get here."

Arne's breakfast churned in his stomach.

His father, a glacialist, was at work two hundred miles north in the Arctic, unaware of what was happening. Arne turned anxiously to Schoolmaster Paulson. "They won't take us to England before Father gets back—they won't— they can't leave him behind alone."

Schoolmaster Paulson's eyes were solemn behind his thick glasses. He snatched his sweater from a peg on the wall. "I'll see what it's all about."

Arne made a rush for the door, pulling on his anorak as he ran.

"Wait, wait for me," Nils yelled.

When they reached the dock, the sysselmann, who governed Spitsbergen for Norway, was ahead of them. A broad-chested man, he stood stolidly at the end of the pier, his gaze riveted on the ships. Next to him waited the director of the mine.

Now the miners streamed down from the coal tunnels that bored into the black cliffs, already snow-crested at the end of August.

Women and children came hurrying along the town's lone street. They were all headed for the dock, to stand against the sharp wind blowing off the fjord, to watch the ships.

Nils pulled the hood of his anorak over his head. "I heard it's warm in England."

England! A faraway, strange land.

England. Without the assurance, the warmth of his

2

father's closeness, the very sound of it made Arne feel hollow. He caught at a straw. "Maybe the British have come to tell us the war is over. Then my father and I can go back to Norway."

Nils took his gaze from the ships for a moment. "They're here because the Nazis are going to invade Spitsbergen, just as they did in Norway." His face was without expression. Only his blue eyes showed what he felt for Arne.

Ugly memories welled up in Arne. The Nazis occupying the country, the resistance, quislings, traitors, pointing fingers and hostages sent to concentration camps.

Arne's father's bold defiance, fighting the occupation as a leader in the Underground. Clever, daring, the Gestapo on his tail—finally too close, too dangerous. The Underground schemed to save his father's life, contriving to get him to Spitsbergen as a member of an international scientific team.

The scheme was successful. The Nazis knew Arne's father only as a glacialist who had spent much time working in Spitsbergen. They became aware too late that a hunted prize had slipped from their grasp.

In Spitsbergen his father had joined the other member of the team, a Swiss scientist.

Out in the fjord, beyond the coal boats, a small vessel plowed a furrow from the battleship to the dock. A murmur ran through the crowd. A cheer as two officers jumped up to the pier.

The sysselmann, the mine director and Schoolmaster Paulson greeted them, shaking hands. Their faces were serious as they walked to the company office.

The crowd was quiet now, waiting.

The rumors: "They've come early. It's because the Nazis are bound to invade before the long darkness sets in. . . ."

3

"It's our radio and weather station they want. . . ." "It's our coal. . . . They're bound to stop our shipments to the Allies. . . ."

It seemed forever to Arne before the officers came out of the company building and returned to the ship.

Men came and went.

Official word passed mouth to mouth: "We leave tomorrow."

Arne felt as if he'd been hit in the stomach. He wormed his way through the crowd, close to the mine office. When the sysselmann came out the door, Arne rushed forward and planted himself in front of him. "My father isn't here. We can't leave without him."

Schoolmaster Paulson stood behind the sysselmann. "Bjørn Kristiansen is not expected to start back for three weeks," he said gently.

The sysselmann's face was grave. "Arne, the ships can't wait. The evacuation must be immediate and secret. Even the Gestapo will not harm a peaceful scientist."

They didn't know. His father would be a prize in the hands of the Nazis. He dared not tell them. He looked up into their faces, the worried sysselmann's, the kind schoolmaster's. Who might be a quisling? A traitor?

"Father has a radio," Arne said desperately. "He could be warned."

The sysselmann shook his head. "Our radio has been silenced. The Nazis would intercept any message we sent. If they should suspect what is happening, they would bomb the ships."

Schoolmaster Paulson put a hand on Arne's shoulder. "Your father is a clever man. He will manage. Get yourself ready to leave."

No one could help him.

Fear, like an electric shock, coursed through his body at the boldness of his scheme.

He had no time to be afraid.

Could he manage it alone?

He must. He remembered the quislings in Norway. He dared not trust anyone, not even Nils.

Nils rushed out of the house at Arne's approach. "Maybe we'll be lucky enough to ride the battleship," he said, eyes shining. It was plain to see that Nils was excited about sailing off to England.

In the house, everything was turmoil.

"Arne," Nils' mother said, "take only the lighter clothing. It doesn't get very cold in England."

Fru Paulson had been good to Arne. She was not demonstrative, but now she put an arm around him. His mother had died when he was very young, and he was self-conscious about her embrace, even though it warmed him. "Remember, Arne, you will be with us in England, the same as here."

He wriggled away, guilty at not telling her his plan. He closed his mind to the guilt.

He began to pack his clothes, all the while mentally cataloging the supplies, the heavy clothing he must spirit away and hide. Where? In one of the mining tunnels high above the town.

His skis were the most important item. They were leaning against the back of the house. He must sneak them up to the mine immediately, before they were locked away in the cellar or shed.

He slipped out of the house, shouldered the skis and was well on his way when he heard a chuckle. Nils.

"You're not going to take them with you. There's no snow in England. What are you up to?"

Arne thought fast. "Hide them. I don't want any Nazi using them."

Nils kept step with him. "Where?"

"Oh, some mine."

"That's stupid," Nils said. "They say the Nazis are going to blow up the mines."

Arne kept walking up the hill. He hoped Nils would drop back.

"You're not making sense," Nils said. He grabbed Arne and spun him around.

"Leave me alone," Arne cried. "Get away from me." He thrust out his arm and punched Nils hard in the jaw.

Nils rocked back and rubbed his face. He looked at Arne, disbelief in his eyes.

Nils was Arne's best friend. Everything that had happened today was too much. Arne felt as if he were crumpling to pieces. He looked at his friend and shook his head. He couldn't speak. He sank to the ground.

Nils crouched beside him. "We all know how you feel, but you heard the sysselmann. He said even the Gestapo would not harm a neutral scientist."

"There's more to it than that, Nils. There's more. . . ." He clamped his lips together. He had said too much. He looked at his friend. He needed to tell his friend. He needed Nils.

Nils' face showed alarm as he listened to Arne's story of his father's work in the resistance.

"If it were your father, what would you do?" Arne asked when he had finished.

"What could I do?" Nils asked.

"What you'd have to do—stay behind when the ships leave."

Nils' eyes widened. "That wouldn't be easy. I'd need help. . . ."

"Yes," Arne said. "Someone to say, when they started looking for you, 'He must be on one of the other ships. He was on the dock.' "

"Ships radio to each other," Nils said.

"The radios will be silent until they're far away."

"What will you do when the ships leave? What's your plan?" Nils asked.

They talked in whispers now.

"I'll stay up at the mine. Keep watch. I'll wait for my father. If the Nazi ships come before he does, then I'll have to go to him."

"That's impossible," Nils exploded. "Two hundred miles with the sun less and less each day and the cold worse and worse. Arne, you haven't been through a winter here on Spitsbergen. You don't know what it's like. Cold, ice a thousand feet deep in places. Glaciers, three months of darkness. How will you find your father?"

"I have a map," Arne said and pulled it from his pocket. "Father marked it for me. He's along this fjord by the great glacial wall at around eighty degrees."

"What about food?"

"There should be some left behind. Then there are trappers' huts along the fjords."

"Some trappers are going with us, those who happened to be here and know about the evacuation."

"Their huts will still be there," Arne argued.

Nils put a finger on a circle on the map. It was marked: Trapper Hans Braun.

"Do you know him?" Arne asked.

"Nobody really knows him. I saw him once. He's a kind

9

of hermit. His hut is about halfway to where your father is. But he's weird, they say."

Nils looked worried.

The worry spilled over to Arne. "I shouldn't have gotten you into this," he said. "You'll get into trouble. Nils, I'm scared—my plan's no good."

"You can't stop now," Nils said. He grabbed the skis Arne had thrown to the ground and got to his feet. "No one can ski as well as you. That will be important. You might make it. Sure, I'll be in big trouble." He grinned. "It won't be the first time."

Nils' assurance caught fire in Arne. He jumped up. "When the war is over, we'll have yarns to swap."

"Right. You'll brag about the bears you fought. I'll tell about the bombs that missed me," Nils said. His words were joking, but his voice was rough. He turned away quickly, and, shouldering Arne's skis, headed for the mine.

Arne followed close behind his friend.

They were in big trouble, both of them.

❊ 3 ❊

What was wrong?

Why didn't the battleship leave?

For what seemed forever, Arne crouched in the mouth of the coal mine and waited, tense, fearful.

The two destroyers had maneuvered out of sight.

The battleship's siren had long since shrieked its readiness to sail.

Still, it did not move.

Had they discovered he was not on any of the ships?

They'd gotten the truth out of Nils! Any second now, they would lower boats and come to get him, force him to go to England.

He began to perspire and then to shiver uncontrollably.

Abruptly the ship gave three short shrieks that sent a jolt through him.

The ship began to move—slowly at first, then faster, faster.

The backdrop of black mountains like heaps of coal, the blue water, the hundreds of gulls sweeping and diving low over the ship made the evacuation unreal. There was no hint that an entire town was fleeing the enemy.

The ship was moving rapidly now. His last tie with the world grew smaller, smaller.

He was alone.

ALONE! The awfulness of his solitude crashed over him. What had he done?

He began to run in the direction the ship was going. He waved frantically. "Wait for me," he screamed. "WAIT! Nils, NILS, tell your father—don't leave me here alone—it's Arne. . . ."

In his terror he stumbled and fell. He rolled. Faster and faster he rolled and tumbled down the hillside. Finally, he lay still, bruised and breathless.

He looked up. The sea was empty. Nothing stirred.

Never before had he been so alone.

His breath came in short, fearful gasps.

His legs and arms felt paralyzed. He'd never be able to move again.

He heard a clucking and turned his head. A covey of feather-legged grouse came pecking along the hillside. There was something alive besides himself, something familiar. "Hello," he said weakly.

The grouse paid no attention. They were unafraid. Arne's father had told him that the wildlife on Spitsbergen had not learned to be afraid of man. He felt better for the company of the grouse and for having talked—having heard the sound of his own voice.

On his feet, he turned from the sea. He could not bear to go down to the empty town. Not yet. He took his flashlight from the pocket of his anorak and plunged into the black silence of the mine. He walked over the bumpy iron rails to the place behind a coal car where he had hidden his supplies. They were just as he and Nils had left them—skis, rucksack, gloves, overgloves, tools, extra clothing. The two most vital items, his compass and map, were in the inside pocket of his anorak.

His wristwatch showed it was almost noon. He began to worry. What if the Nazis had arrived?

He went cautiously into the daylight.

There was nothing.

He would go down to the town. Busy himself with things that must be done, find the key to the Paulson house which Nils had hidden away for him.

By the time he climbed down the mountainside a wind had blown up, scattering the light covering of snow on the town's single street. Already the eerie feeling of a ghost town hung in the air. The crunch of the overhead coal gondolas was silenced, the school, church, houses—shuttered, boarded up. The sandy plot where he and Nils had played soccer with friends was sad in its desertion.

Nils' house looked strange, unfamiliar, desolate.

An alien sound vibrated from the sky.

Nazi planes?

He flattened himself against the side of the house and looked up.

A huge flock of geese was passing overhead, followed by a second flock, this one lower in the sky. The air was filled with gabbling.

13

The migration south had begun.

Arne imagined their flight over the Arctic Ocean and the Norwegian Sea. Maybe they'd fly right over Oslo. Would he ever see his old home again? Homesickness wrenched through him as he watched the smooth, orderly flight of the wild geese.

A young straggler lagged. "Honk! Honk!"

To Arne it sounded like a desperate cry. "Help! Help!"

"GO! GO!" Arne shouted to the gosling. "You'll make it."

He watched the straggler reach the flock. Good, he's with all the others.

And then Arne remembered something. His father's rule of the Arctic was never travel alone.

❄ 4 ❄

Each morning Arne scanned the sea.

Each day the temperature dropped.

Each day the sun stayed a shorter time.

But the Nazi ships did not come.

He became bolder in his thinking as the days passed. The Germans would not come with the long night approaching. They would wait until spring to invade.

Why sleep in the mine? He moved his skis and all his supplies into Nils' father's house.

His hopes rose. It was now just a little more than two weeks until his father would start back. They would stay here until the dark months passed. When the ice melted in the fjords, they would find a small boat; they would escape. . . .

The German destroyer came on the seventh day.

Arne saw it from the same window he had seen the British ships. For a paralyzing instant all the feeling went out of his legs. They felt hollow, rubbery.

Then he moved automatically, with speed and precision, as he had rehearsed in his mind many times.

His rucksack was ready, with food and a thermos of hot tea. In moments it was on his back, his skis over his shoulder. He was on his way, trying to stay out of sight of the ship in the harbor.

The terrain was flat, crisscrossed by a network of small rivers. He would be exposed and visible for miles. He hugged the riverbanks and took refuge in the bends. The men on the ship would be sure to scan the area with binoculars. He could feel them burn into his back like eagles' eyes. He moved fast, but he felt as if he were living a nightmare. Running in one spot, not getting anywhere. Any moment now he would hear a round of shots from the ship's guns.

Not until he was several miles upvalley did he have any feeling of safety. He had been there before, the last time with his father. As he remembered the day, his aloneness was suddenly sharp and hurting. It had been midsummer, when the sun never sets in the Arctic. A three-month day without night, when grasses and wild flowers—bluebells, glacier crowfeet, reindeer roses—burst from the rocky land. His father knew all the growing things. He had picked a stem of oval leaves. "Scurvy-wort. The vitamin C of the Arctic. Men have died of scurvy with this plant growing practically under the soles of their boots."

Arne had run a finger over a leaf. "Why didn't they eat some?"

"They didn't know. It takes knowledge and patience to survive here."

Patience!

Arne had no time for patience now. His father would start back to Longyearbyen in fourteen days. To stop him, Arne must travel two hundred miles in thirteen days. The fourteenth day would be too late. Speed was the thing. For that he needed snow so he could ski. But there were only patches of it in the valley. The wind had swept the stony land almost bare.

This was a worry. But when he struggled to the crest of the mountain, he gazed into an endless white world of snowy plains, icy peaks, glittering glaciers. It was vast, boundless—a formidable enemy.

Fearful, he wanted to turn back. But the Nazi enemy was behind him. There was just one thing to do—go on.

He buckled on his skis. Suddenly he felt he was being watched. His neck muscles tensed. He pivoted slowly and searched the whiteness.

There, not twenty feet away, a fox stood against a snowbank, barely visible in its white coat. Arne let out his breath. "Well, hello there, Fox," he called, delighted to see something alive.

The fox stood motionless and ignored him.

"Well, I'm on my way," Arne said. He jabbed his ski poles into the snow and forged ahead.

Arne was sure of himself on skis. He felt that sureness— confidence—now. With the wind at his back, he raced effortlessly down the slopes. As he bent to the contour of the land, his skis were an extension of his feet, a part of the rhythm of muscle and bone.

17

Even though the wind was cold, he felt warm and, after a while, thirsty. He stopped in the lee of a boulder, took off his rucksack and stretched his arm and back muscles. He took from his pack the thermos of hot tea and drank sparingly, then filled the thermos to the top with snow.

He was ready to be off again when he sensed something moving.

He turned. The fox froze to a stop behind him.

"So you've been trailing me."

The fox took no notice.

"You're looking for company, same as I."

When Arne began to climb the hill ahead, the fox shot forward with long, graceful leaps, white against white, a ghostly fox.

"Good-bye," Arne yelled after him.

But when he reached the brow of the hill, the fox stood waiting, brown eyes glittering.

Arne propelled himself forward. "I'll beat you on the downhill," he shouted.

Partway down the slope he turned and stopped. The fox leaped and swam in the snow.

Arne leaned on his poles and waited for the fox to catch up. "Aren't you afraid of me?" he asked the fox. "Maybe I've got a gun. You might end up lining the hood of an anorak. You shouldn't trust people."

The fox lay down panting on the snow.

Their shadows on the snow were yards long and close.

"On your feet, Fox," Arne said.

There was no time to waste.

<mark>## ⁂ 5 ⁂</mark>

It was midafternoon, and nearly dark, when Arne reached the edge of Sassen Fjord. The fox had stayed with him.

Arne pulled the map from his anorak and unfolded it to study the black dots which pinpointed the huts and creep-ins of trappers. They were roughly ten to fifteen miles apart. The fox followed as he moved, searching.

He was lucky. It did not take long to find a tar-papered shack. It was really just a refuge hut, and it sat somewhat dizzily on a rise close to the shore. Arne shoved open the door to a single, smoke-blackened room. The ceiling was barely high enough for a man to stand. One wall was caved

19

in. Bear . . . Arne thought nervously. A big ice bear.

Still, it was shelter. The first thing to do was build a fire. As Arne headed for the shore to find wood, the fox was gone.

The sky over the water was noisy with seabirds. The beach was strewn with a jumble of things the sea had coughed up: planks, boxes, trunks of trees, driftwood bleached white. Sandpipers scattered as he approached.

The logs Arne gathered shone as if polished by their journey through polar seas. Where had they come from? he wondered. What continent? Which country?

He spied the fox running light-footed along the shore, his bushy tail streaming out behind him. The fox was looking for his supper. Arne must look for his.

It took three of his precious matches to get a fire going. It roared and spewed out inky smoke before steadying.

His father had told Arne the code of the trapper: wood and food of some kind must always be left in a hut. The last person to stay in this one must have been poor. All Arne found was a paper bag of pressed oatmeal. Still, it would make a hot meal. He'd leave something in exchange. Pemmican, he decided.

The only cooking utensil was a blackened frying pan. It would do to melt snow in which to cook the oats.

The warmth of the fire and the bubbling porridge gave the shack a homey feeling. He'd celebrate the good start of his trip. He opened one of the cans of condensed milk he had brought. It was frozen, and, after he thawed it, grainy, but it was still good. He allowed himself a heaping teaspoon of sugar to sprinkle over the gruel.

He thought of his friend Nils. He wished he were here. Was he in trouble on Arne's account?

Arne had just finished the meal when he heard an eerie

shrieking. He rushed outside to see terns diving at the fox, which had dragged a dead fish from the waves. With crafty aim, the birds shot down on him. The fox let out a thin, anguished yap as their sharp beaks ripped his fur. He flipped over on his back and struck out desperately with his paws.

Arne grabbed one of his ski poles from alongside the hut. "Thieves," he yelled and swung the pole around in a circle over his head. The marauding birds scattered. "Thieves, go find your own food."

The fox dragged his prize a distance from Arne, as if he too might steal it.

A strange blue light touched the icy mountains and snowy ground. The moon, a luminous disk, seemed close enough to grasp.

Finished with his food, the fox drew closer to the hut. He lay down, curled into a circle, tail over snout.

As Arne turned to go inside, a mist obscured the moon. He remembered his father saying, "Only one thing you can count on about Arctic weather. It's fickle."

Later, in his sleeping bag, he heard the wind whine mournfully through the cave-in the bear had made. He shivered. He did not want to meet up with a bear.

He heard the fox howl, a piercing, sad sound. Far away, a howl answered. Then all was quiet.

Arne wondered how many huts he would sleep in before he reached his father.

He started at every new sound. What if the bear came back?

He was afraid to go to sleep.

His eyes were heavy. He was snug and warm in his reindeer sleeping bag.

He was asleep.

❋ 6 ❋

Arne awakened to a strange sight. The walls of the hut were white with hoarfrost. The temperature had dropped.

He yawned and stretched, and then he was on his feet. Even before he pulled on his boots and sweater, he opened the door. The fox was gone. He had expected as much, but he had a sense of loss. The fox had been company, someone to talk to.

It would take too much time to get the stove fired up again, so Arne drank a small amount of the hot tea he had poured into his thermos the night before, ate cold sausage and some biscuits.

He studied his map while he ate. The fjord waters that

lay north resembled, roughly, a left hand, palm down, fingers thrust into the terrain.

He traced the route he had traveled the day before. He was now past the base of the "first finger." From here he would be traveling over flatland along the fjord. He had made some twenty-five miles yesterday. If he averaged that much each day, it should take him eight days, in all, to reach his father's camp at the edge of a great glacial wall.

He drew a circle around the next hut marked on the map. It was a distance of about thirty miles. He would make it by nightfall.

Pocketing the map, he eased his shoulders into his rucksack and went outside. As he strapped on his skis and slid down to the fjord, he looked for the tracks of the fox. Fresh snow had obliterated them. He was moving in a silent, white world. The only sound was the long scraping of his skis.

At noon, pleased with his progress, Arne halted close by a lagoon, unfastened his rucksack and took from it dried fruit and crackers.

As he ate, he watched eiderducks fly close to the water, then glide down to join others snuggled like a feathery quilt across the pond. Migrating! "So you're leaving," he said out loud, for he needed to hear a voice, even his own. The ducks murmured drowsily but paid no heed to him.

The brief stop made Arne conscious of the numbing cold. He swung his arms and stamped with his skis. He wiggled his toes to get the circulation going in his feet. He dug in his poles and moved forward.

The sky darkened.

The terrain roughened.

No more easy skiing. He took off his skis to climb over masses of rocks deposited by glaciers.

The temperature kept plunging.

The sea spumed against the shore. A cruel wind blew snow, sharp as needles, against his face and under the hood of his anorak.

Would he ever reach the next hut? He had to find shelter.

He was almost upon it before he saw the sagging cluster of boards, the door banging open. The wreck was completely filled with snow.

It was unbelievable. Too much to comprehend. There was no shelter within thirty miles. Where would he sleep?

The wind, savage now, drove the snow before it in enormous drifts. He could see almost nothing.

BLIZZARD!

Dig in. Fast. No more time.

A snowdrift would have to do.

He struggled out of his rucksack and got his short-handled shovel. As he burrowed, ptarmigan flew out from under the cover of the snow and startled him.

No time to cut blocks of snow, dig a passageway, hollow out a shelter to sit up, lie down.

Falling snow—soon it would clog the opening—ram a ski pole into top of drift, ventilation.

Crawl inside, pull off boots and icy anorak, get into sleeping bag, pull flap over head—numb, exhausted.

Slowly, agonizingly, feeling came back in his fingers, toes. Then warmth, sleepiness. He must sit up, get matches and candle. Save the flashlight batteries. The candle flame was steady; hardly a puff of wind crept into the shelter. Snow was already blocking the opening.

Drink tea—still warm. Food frozen. Put raisins and

chocolate and boots in sleeping bag; they would thaw by morning.

Blow out candle. Listen. Snowhouse muted the rage of the blizzard. Battle of winds, might go on for hours, could rage for days. Fear! Panic! He might be so deeply buried in snow he could not dig himself out. No one knew where he was. Father. He would return to Longyearbyen, be shot. A terrible scream. Whose? His!

Control!

Pull the sleeping bag over head, shut out the storm.

Remember fun. Norway at midsummer, when the lilacs bloom, bonfires, singing, laughter.

Sleep!

✳ 7 ✳

Arne awakened slowly to the darkness and silence.

He reached out. His hands struck a wall of snow.

He remembered. The horror of it brought him fully awake.

He fumbled for his flashlight and looked at his wristwatch. It had stopped at nine o'clock. Morning? Night? What day? How long had he been in this grave? How deeply was he buried?

He lay on his stomach and began to shovel his way through the snow that blocked the opening. Each shovelful had to be thrown behind him in the shelter.

He would never reach the outside.

At the first glimpse of gray light, he felt reborn. He lay gasping, observing the miracle. He burrowed to the outside. The blizzard was over. The nightmare, he decided, had happened just yesterday.

After the warmth of the snowhouse, he felt the rasping cold keenly. He hurried into motion, dug out his belongings. He ate the thawed raisins and chocolate. Then he buckled on his skis and slid down to the fjord. It had iced over during the night.

His map showed he was still about twenty miles from the tip of the fjord's "middle finger" and the next shelter, which, from the size of the circle on the map, was probably just a creep-in.

If he could, however, cross the fjord at this point, he would be close by the hut of the trapper Hans Braun, the hermit that Nils had told him about. If he went all the way around the fjord, it was some sixty miles. If he crossed the fjord, he would save at least two days' journey. This was important. He had made only ten miles yesterday.

He crossed to the edge of the ice and prodded it with a ski pole. Water bubbled up.

Too thin.

He'd have to go the long way.

At first there were stretches along the shore where he rhythmically thrust his poles into the snow and his skis swished smoothly over the surface. But those stretches became rarer as the morning wore on. Often he had to make wide circles around cliffs that rose starkly from the sea.

Again and again, detours slowed him.

At noon he ate only crackers with a mouthful of snow to quench his thirst. He knew this was foolhardy. Cold in the stomach took away energy. But he was impatient to be on his way.

The frozen fjord was tempting. The other side seemed so close. He'd test the ice once more. He put his weight on it. It held.

He stabbed it with his ski pole.

Thick.

Should he risk it?

At the rate he was traveling, he'd never reach his father on time. He needed the two days he would save by crossing the ice.

He was already tired, miserable. Across the fjord there was a trapper, a warm hut.

On skis, if one moved fast and did not stop, even thin ice held.

The sky began to cloud over.

Another blizzard?

He'd try the ice.

He jabbed his poles into it and thrust forward.

The wind was at his back. The ice was smooth as silk. He raced, thrilling.

He was in control.

Confident.

There was nothing to fear.

Until halfway across the fjord, he felt the ice begin to sway. Slowly, up and down it heaved.

He heard an ominous cracking.

With horror he saw a narrow lead fill with black water. Speed carried him over it.

He was safe.

Then he heard a loud grinding, gnashing explosion. All around him the ice broke into giant slabs.

Frantically he jabbed his ski poles into the slab he stood on, while ice blocks smashed each other with a crashing roar.

His only chance to survive would be if the current pressed the ice floes against the land to make a bridge.

A tremendous block crashed into his floe and almost jolted him into the water. He could not keep his balance. His rucksack weighted him down. He cast it off into the sea of ice and lunged forward with all his strength, around cracks, across the weaving floes.

A lead opened and widened in the last stretch of ice before the shore. A cracking bent the ice beneath his flying skis.

Desperately he tore open his anorak and held it wide to the wind, making a sail. He shot across the open water and catapulted onto the icy bank, limp, gasping.

Only his ski tracks proved he had crossed the impossible ice pack.

His rucksack was gone.

His hands in his mittens were lumps of ice.

He must find the hut of Trapper Braun soon.

With numb fingers he managed to get his compass from his pocket. This far north it might not be accurate. He'd follow its direction nonetheless.

His legs were as stiff as ski poles.

His eyelashes were frozen together.

He dragged on, frozen, barely conscious.

A light!

Or was it a star?

Stars were not square.

He brushed the ice from his face.

A hut.

He was almost there. Another few steps.

From out of nowhere something white and furry lunged at him.

A bear?

He fell to the ground.

"Kara," he heard a gruff voice shout.

A giant stood silhouetted in the doorway of the hut, a gun in his hand.

The white world turned black.

❄ 8 ❄

Arne jerked upright.

Where was he?

A hut, rough, smoke-blackened.

He craned his neck to look into the bunk above him.
Empty.

The room was warm, filled with the smell of coffee.
There was a table, two stools and little else.

Now he remembered. The beast, the giant with a gun.
The trapper Hans Braun. He fell back on the bunk. He was
safe.

His bones ached. He could go on sleeping forever.

The door burst open, and freezing air whooshed in.

31

Through half-closed eyelids he saw the giant. His shaggy head just missed the ceiling. His face was covered with so much hair, he looked more troll than man.

The giant did not glance at Arne.

Arne watched him toss his gun on a shelf, then go to the stove and dump a fish into a frying pan. When he took off his anorak, Arne saw the width of the man's back—big muscles moving under a thick shirt.

When the fish was cooked, he flipped it right onto the table. He set the coffeepot alongside it, then slammed a loaf of bread down and stabbed it with an oversize knife.

He turned abruptly. For the first time he acknowledged Arne. "Alive, are you?" he growled. "Then sit up and eat."

Arne slid from the bunk. His stomach felt queer. He looked at the food. He was going to be sick. He looked away.

"From what fine place have you come that you turn your nose up?" the trapper asked.

"My home is in Oslo."

"Ho! From Oslo. So we have fine manners. Well, here we do not eat for pleasure. We eat to survive."

He cut a hunk of bread from the loaf and shoved it across to Arne. Then he grasped the coffeepot in a hand big as a bear paw and drank from the spout, mockery in his deep-set eyes.

It was unreal. The trapper seemed an actor playing a part. Nils had said the man was strange.

Arne tasted the fish. It was better than it looked. Now he was ravenous. He reached for more bread.

"Takk for maten," he said when the meal was finished.

The trapper did not answer his thank-you with the usual *Velbekomme*. He stabbed a toothpick between his teeth and

32

fixed a hypnotic eye on Arne. "How is it you came here half-dead?"

Arne felt his face redden with embarrassment.

"I took a shortcut across the fjord. I thought the ice would hold."

The trapper chewed on his toothpick. "Why are you here alone?"

Arne squirmed under his gaze. "I'm on my way to see" —something in the trapper's eyes stopped him—"to see a friend," he finished lamely.

"A friend? And where is this friend?"

Arne was on guard. "North. . . ."

"How far?"

Arne shrank from the questioning, but the trapper's eyes bored into him, demanded answers.

"From here—maybe a hundred miles."

The trapper laughed—a derisive sound. "IGNOMIN-IOUS," he shouted. "You intend to travel that far north? A stupid boy who tries to cross thin ice and has already lost his provisions? The winter is almost at hand, and yet you are headed toward the Pole—to see a friend. Where did you start this crazy journey?"

Arne's face grew hot, but he stifled his anger. He needed the man's help. "From Longyearbyen. I have a map. I have money. I can pay if you will give me supplies."

"MONEY!" Hans sputtered. He roared that word again: "IGNOMINIOUS! What is money here? When did you begin this journey?"

"Three days ago."

The trapper crossed his arms over his wide chest and glared. "Let's have the truth. Longyearbyen was evacuated."

33

Arne was caught.

"Out with it. Why were you left?"

"I didn't want to go. I hid when the ships left."

"Why did you do such a stupid thing?"

Arne squirmed in his chair. "Because, because of my— friend. He wouldn't know what had happened."

"This friend—what is he doing up north?"

"He's a glacialist."

"A scientific man. He should be able to take care of himself and not need the help of a boy."

Arne swallowed his anger and pride. "Will you help me?" he asked again.

The trapper's eyes seemed to bore straight through Arne. "Not until you tell me the whole truth. Then I'll think about it."

Arne felt as if his insides were crumbling. How could he tell this stranger about his father? He wished he had more experience at judging people. How could one tell who was a quisling, a traitor?

The trapper shrugged. Turned away.

Arne had to tell if he were to have help. He blurted, "I'm going to my father. The Gestapo hunted him in Norway. He escaped. If he returns to Longyearbyen and they get hold of him, they'll put him in prison camp or worse. . . ."

The trapper's eyes glinted. "His name?"

"Bjørn Kristiansen," Arne gasped, with what seemed to him his last breath. He rubbed his eyes.

The trapper's face was expressionless. He pushed away from the table, hauled a rucksack from a shelf and tossed it to Arne. "It needs repairs. You can have a sleeping bag and what supplies you need."

Arne was too overcome with thankfulness to express it in

words. Now he had a friend. He set to work immediately on the rucksack. "I must be ready tomorrow."

"In the Arctic the weather decides such things," the trapper said. "You have a map showing where your father is." He held out his hand. "Give it to me."

Arne stiffened.

At that moment there was a scratching at the door.

"Kara," the trapper said and opened it.

A huge white dog bounded into the room.

"So that's the beast that attacked me last night!" Arne said. "I thought it was a bear."

"Attacked! Huskies love man."

Kara made a leap at Arne, almost knocking him to the floor. She licked his face. Nuzzled him.

Arne wrestled with the dog. Thanks to Kara, the trapper seemed to have forgotten about the map.

Later, when the trapper left the hut, Arne took the map from the pocket of his anorak and hid it inside his shirt.

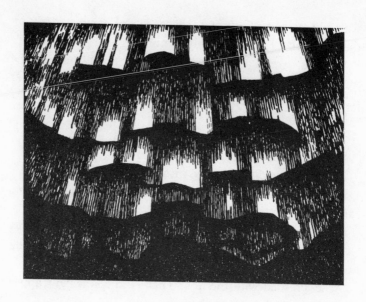

❋ 9 ❋

Kara kept Arne company while he repaired the rucksack and stored in it the supplies Hans gave him. He sharpened tools and tarred skis.

The dog nuzzled Arne as he worked, teasing for attention.

Arne took Kara's head into his hands. "You're curious about me, same as the trapper," he said. "You'd like to pester me with questions, too."

Hans had pulled too much information out of Arne. Still, he reasoned, if someone fell into my hut half-dead, asking for help, I'd ask questions, too.

He got to his feet. "Let's see how these skis feel. Come on, Kara."

With the dog bounding at his side, Arne skied toward the fjord.

The regular order of day and night was changing. The stony land was passing into the long night. The sun was later each day in bobbing up over the horizon, and its course was shorter. There was only dawn and twilight. It was almost noon, and the sun was just rising. Again he counted the days he had left to reach his father. HURRY seemed burned into his brain.

In the distance, he saw the trapper, hand on the stock of his gun.

Silently, with just a gentle swish of his skis, Arne came closer.

A seal lay on the ice in the pale sunlight.

The trapper had a perfect shot at it.

He was taking too long.

Kara bounded to the shore. Barked.

Instantly the seal disappeared into a hole in the ice.

Arne laughed as he skied down to Hans.

Hans turned, raised a fist. "Ignominious," he shouted. "We could have had fresh meat."

Arne knew it had not been his or the dog's fault that the seal had escaped.

Hans' beard was covered with hoarfrost. He looked like a wild man. "The seal's blood would have given us energy for our journey tomorrow."

Arne stiffened. "OUR journey?"

It was the trapper's turn to laugh. "I'm going to make sure you don't fall through ice again."

"I don't need a bodyguard," Arne spat out.

The trapper turned toward the hut. "I have traplines to repair north along the fjord. For that distance I'll see you don't get into trouble."

Arne knew Hans' plan was sensible. The trapper knew the area. He could save Arne much time. But he felt uneasy. Why had Hans missed the seal? Trappers never missed.

And the word *ignominious*. A strange word for a trapper. The trappers Arne had known at Longyearbyen sometimes used colorful language. They swore. They would never say "ignominious."

Arne shrugged off the worry. He should be thankful for the trapper's help. What would he have done without Hans?

❄ 10 ❄

NIGHTMARE!

Arne was running, fast and away from the trapper.

But his feet stayed in one place.

Terror!

The trapper reached out, grabbed him.

Arne jerked awake.

Hans was shaking him.

"Weather's good," he said. "Time to be on our way. Eggs are ready."

"Eggs?" Arne said, trying to shake off the dream, sliding out of his bunk.

"Gulls' eggs. Saved since the laying season. I keep them

frozen in a glacier. They'll give us energy for the trip. Sit, boy, they've been boiling away for almost half an hour and are done."

The egg Hans set before him was enormous. Arne tried to crack it. The shell was like cement.

"Don't spare your muscles. Give it a bang on the side with your knife," Hans instructed.

Arne gagged a little at the transparent white of the egg. He managed to swallow it.

"I've some chores," Hans said. "You saw up some frozen meat for Kara. Then chain her. We'll leave soon as I get back."

"Chain her?"

"She'll slow us."

"That's cruel," Arne said.

The trapper nodded. "It's a cruel land."

He took his gun from the shelf. There was a strange gleam in his eyes as he ran his fingers down the barrel. "Would you rather I shot her?"

The trapper stamped out, and Arne patted Kara. Then he took seal meat and a saw outside and began to cut it into pieces. He threw a few to Kara. And then he stared. The trapper's ski tracks were etched plainly in the snow.

Something about them worried Arne.

Where had he seen such tracks before? They had not been made by Norwegian skis.

A picture flashed into his mind. He was skiing with his father outside Oslo. His father pointed to ski tracks. "German," he pronounced.

All of the things that had bothered him about Hans now raced through Arne's mind. The trapper's way of speaking. His Norwegian was different from that spoken in Norway, not the same as in Spitsbergen. He had wormed out of Arne information about his father, information Arne had been determined to tell no one. He had known about the evacuation, yet radios were silent. Did Hans really have traplines? Was he going to them? If so, why would he not take Kara?

Pure terror washed over Arne. He had been about to lead this stranger to his father. He had been a fool.

Feverishly now he prepared to leave.

He grabbed his rucksack and all his supplies from the hut. He buckled on his skis.

Kara sensed his panic. She raced about, excited. She jumped up, putting her paws on Arne's shoulders.

Had Hans been joking about shooting the dog?

Kara trembled in her eagerness.

"You want to go with me, don't you? Well, why not?"

He thrust the seal meat he had sawed for her into his rucksack.

"We'll have to move fast. Let's go."

He dug his poles into the snow.

He was off.

The dog raced on ahead.

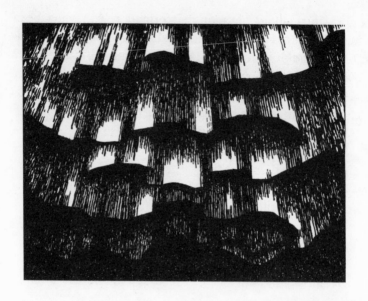

Arne had an eerie feeling that he was being followed. Again and again he broke his fast pace to search the frozen landscape.

Nothing!

He was making such good time on the flatlands along the fjord that he began to relax. His spirits soared. The going was easy. He sang to Kara. She seemed to understand. "We'll see Father sooner than I thought," he told her as they halted at the base of a steep cliff which blocked the shoreline. "Now we'll eat."

Kara snuggled up against him, tilting her head sideways, watching.

"Imagine how surprised he'll be to see us."

Kara nudged him.

He reached down and tugged at her heavy coat. "You're hungry. Is that what you're saying?"

Kara wagged her tail enthusiastically.

Arne gave her some of the seal meat. "I should have taken time to saw more. But when we get to Kings Bay, we'll get some."

Kara was finished with the food in seconds. Arne threw her a piece of the pemmican he was chewing. He scanned the trail behind him. Safe. "Let's go," he said.

Kara beat Arne easily on the climb up the cliff. With a smug look on her face, she waited for him on the crest of the ridge.

A glacier gleamed ahead. Wedged between twin peaks, the congealed river was a frozen highway. Northward rose an eternity of ice mountains. The sun was a flaming circle low over the horizon. How soon would it disappear altogether?

HURRY!

Arne dug in his poles and flew on the wind. As he followed the smooth curve of the glacier, he was constantly on the alert for concealed crevasses, for the grayish look of indented snow, a warning that wind and pressure had bridged over the top of a split.

There were ravines to skirt and boulders of ice at the glacier's sides to stay clear of. The way was strange, uncanny, exhilarating, but he felt in control. Nothing could stop him now.

He had not reckoned with Kara.

She could not keep up with him on the downhills. He waited for her time and again.

That night they slept in a creep-in, huddled together.

Arne had given the dog the last of the seal meat. "We'll be in Kings Bay tomorrow. By noon," he promised her.

But by noon that day they had traveled only half the distance to Kings Bay.

The cold was intense, the wind violent. It tore into the hood of his anorak and bit into his ears. It surrounded him, grabbing from all sides. At times it seemed to cut the skis from under him.

By late afternoon it wound down. Still, they had not reached Kings Bay.

Arne felt despair. He was tired and so was the dog. They moved slowly, clumsily.

It was night when they stood on a knoll and looked down at the village, a crescent along the shore. On the snow, gleaming under a polished moon, everything stood out plainly—houses, mine buildings.

Arne reached down and patted Kara where she lay panting in the snow. "Down there we'll get food, and I'll have a warm place to sleep."

But something was wrong.

There were no lights.

No smoke came from chimneys.

With a sinking feeling that gave way to nausea, he realized the town was deserted.

Then he saw a figure moving on skis.

Joyfully he started down the slope.

A big hulk emerged from the shadows. Familiar.

Kara ran toward the skier.

Arne shifted his weight, turned his skis abruptly to stop. THE TRAPPER!

"Kara," Arne cried as he dug his poles into the snow and lunged in the opposite direction.

"Stop," Hans shouted.

44

Arne hurtled down the incline and across the frozen fjord.

A quick glance behind. The trapper was trailing.

Faster! FASTER!

A cliff loomed ahead.

Skis sideways, Arne climbed to a crest, then slid onto a glacier, a narrow ice road hemmed in by gigantic ice boulders.

Kara sprang ahead.

Arne glanced behind. The trapper was not in sight.

But Arne had failed to see the slight depression ahead, the grayness. Danger signal, CREVASSE!

Too late he felt the air roar up. At the same moment Kara made a gigantic leap over the abyss, Arne's skis struck at the edge. He plunged down.

He crunched to a sickening stop, one ski wedged against the wall of ice.

He clawed the sides of the crevasse, trying to grip and pull himself up. His mittened hands slid off the slippery wall.

Above his head he heard Kara's whimper. He could not see her.

How far down in the ice slit was he?

He tried to free his ski. Slowly, agonizingly, he did, only to slide down another foot. The ski caught again.

He was going to fall to the bottom of the crevasse.

He beat at the ice, flailed his arms and thrashed. Still he slid.

The cold crept into his bones. He must rest. Then try again.

He thought of his family, of his father, his long-ago father. He had called him "Papa."

His mother. Strange how he remembered her clearly

now. She was helping him build a snow troll. He heard her laughter . . . soft, chuckly. She sang him to sleep sometimes. He would sleep now.

From far off he heard a whimper.

Kara. Why was Kara whimpering?

Suddenly a light blinded him.

"ARNE! ARNE!"

The trapper's face loomed above him, casting a shadow.

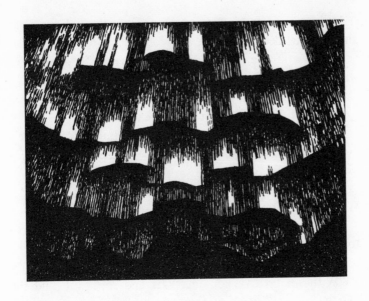

❄ 12 ❄

Arne expected jeers, mockery.

"Hang on," Hans shouted. "I'll drop a rope."

Arne lunged for it. The pain in his arms brought life back to his body.

"Can you knot it around you?" Hans shouted down.

Slowly, with numb fingers, Arne managed the knot.

Then, agonizingly, he felt himself hauled to the surface.

Hans untied the knot. He did not rage at Arne. "Are you in one piece?" he asked.

"I think so," Arne said, untangling himself from skis and rope.

He staggered to his feet, and pain shot through his right ankle. It buckled under him.

Across, on the other side of the crevasse, Kara ran wildly.

"Lie down," Hans yelled.

Obediently the dog groveled in the snow.

"We've got to get over to that side," Hans said. "There's no way to get around the crevasse. There are ice bulges along both sides."

Arne limped to the edge of the dark slit. "It's not so wide. We could make a running jump."

"The way you're limping? We need a bridge. We'll have to make one."

"With what?"

"With what we've got. Our skis and rope. I'll bind the two pairs together. You toss our backpacks to the other side."

Arne watched as Hans lashed the skis double, knotted his rope and placed the "bridge" over the narrowest part of the crevasse. It looked flimsy over the dark abyss. He held his breath as Hans crawled out and flattened himself on the skis.

"Climb over me," Hans ordered. "It's the only way to be sure you won't slip."

Arne was too scared to think. He did as he was told.

Slowly, slowly, he crept on his hands and knees over the prostrate Hans.

Freezing air surged up from the black depths of the crevasse with a ghostly whine. The blood pounded in his ears, and, after an eternity, he was on the other side.

In terror he watched the big man crawl forward and off the ski bridge to regain his feet.

Kara greeted them as if they'd come back from the grave.

Hans untied the skis. "If you can ski down to the fjord, we'll make a sled for you."

It was a slow, painful journey. At the bottom there was an abandoned hut. When they reached it, Hans ripped planks from the sagging door. "We'll use your skis for the runners."

Kara, meanwhile, raced in circles. "Huskies like to pull. She knows something's up," Hans said.

"She's hungry," Arne said. "I ran out of food for her."

"It's not a long run. She'll make it all right. I'll fix her a make-do rope harness."

Arne marveled at the trapper's ingenuity with the few tools he had. Finally, he watched him tie a rope for steering at the end of the crude sled. He remembered his father's words about knowledge and patience being necessary to survive in the Arctic.

Kara was wild with excitement, ready to be off.

Hans packed the sledge with their rucksacks.

"All right, Arne, get on," he said.

Arne hobbled onto the sled.

"Go, Kara," Hans shouted.

Off they soared, the trapper alongside shouting commands: "Left, steady, right."

Arne's ankle did not hurt as much now that he was off it. As he lay snug and warm on the sled, he felt overwhelming gratitude toward Hans.

How could he have doubted the motives of the trapper? He had saved his life twice, even risked his own.

"HALT!" The trapper's voice rang out as they approached a hut built on a rise along the fjord. Even in the darkness, Arne could tell that this was a strong hut. The moon hung over it like a lantern, close and big, silvering the snow on the roof.

49

After he had limped inside and the trapper had lighted a lamp, he saw that the hut was clean and well cared for. There was kindling, logs, coal.

Soon a fire was blazing in the stove and water was boiling in the kettle.

"How is it that we can use any hut?" Arne asked.

"It goes back a thousand years. King Øystein of Norway decreed the death sentence for the ones who did not leave a hut in the same condition they found it. It's a matter of survival. And now, let's have a look at your ankle."

Arne had a hard time getting off the right boot. "Swollen," Hans said as he probed gently. "No bones broken. I'll get a bucket of snow, and we'll put on some cold compresses."

By the time that was done and Kara had been fed, tea was ready, and Hans brought Arne a mugful.

"Takk," Arne said. He felt guilty, ashamed, for all the trouble he had caused Hans. "Why aren't you angry?" he asked.

Hans shrugged. "I was young once. I understand impatience. You were in a hurry to reach your father."

"Why didn't you abandon me? Why did you follow me?"

"You had my dog."

Arne reached down and petted Kara, who was lying at his feet. What had made him even think Hans would harm the dog? Remorseful, he was about to say so, but the trapper was on his feet. "We must have a feast to celebrate your safety."

The feast turned out to be a can of fish balls and flatbread. It did indeed taste like a feast.

The hut was cozy in the lamplight. A bearskin was nailed to the wall. The bunks were covered with deerskin pelts. Black-and-white drawings of peaked mountains and frozen

seas were on the walls. There was a shelf of books. Another shelf held a row of bears carved from driftwood.

The hut, Arne thought, was that of an educated man.

It had been a long day. Arne's eyes were heavy. He climbed into bed. He thought about tomorrow. Would his ankle be strong enough to travel? He had maybe seventy more miles to go. At twenty miles or so each day, he would see his father in three days.

Tomorrow he would show Hans the map. Hans would help him plot the way.

Tomorrow . . .

❋ 13 ❋

Arne had a nightmare.

An ice bear, towering over the cabin, banged against the roof with huge paws.

He awakened with a start. Jerked upright.

BANG! There it was again.

"Bear . . ." he yelled down to the trapper, who was stoking the stove.

"Just the wind slamming scraps of corrugated iron around the chimney," Hans said.

Arne came fully awake. He swung out of bed. Slid to the floor. Pain, like fire, shot through his ankle.

"A bad morning," Hans growled. "The wind is from the east. We're in for some unweather."

"Unweather?"

"You'll see."

Arne limped to the window. All he could see was snow flashing against it. Everything in the hut rattled.

"Sit," Hans said. "This morning it's oatmeal. There's yeast in the cupboard but no bread."

Arne bolted his breakfast.

"Let me have a look at your ankle," Hans said.

"It's better," Arne said. "It won't slow me today."

"Today?" Hans exploded. "You're not going anywhere today on that ankle and in this weather."

"Look," Arne said, pulling up his pants leg. "The swelling is down. I'm used to storms. We have them in Norway."

Hans pounded a fist on the table. "You just think you know storms. You'll not travel today. Maybe not for a week. But then again, maybe in a day or two."

Arne pushed away from the table. "I must go."

"Going now would be a waste of energy," Hans said. "Here we learn to conserve energy."

"I can't just sit when every day counts," Arne shouted.

"All right," Hans said calmly. "Go. But first, bring in wood. You'll find it, all cut, on the west side of the hut. Take a sack to drag it."

Arne's ankle began to thump when he pulled on his boots. It would stop.

He put on sweater, anorak, gloves, and made for the outdoors.

The wind grabbed him the second he was out of the hut. It came from all directions. It cut his legs from under him. He stumbled. His ankle throbbed.

53

By the time he reached the wood, ice crystals clung to his face, and his hands in his mittens were stiff.

The wind had swept the wood clean of snow, but it took an eternity to fill the sack and drag it into the hut. He stumbled inside, exhausted, his lungs aching. He fell into a chair, gasping.

Hans handed him a mug of steaming cocoa. "How soon you leaving?"

Arne gritted his teeth. "You win."

"It's early for this kind of storm," Hans said. "It could die down by tomorrow. Don't worry too much. I know safe shortcuts." He grinned. "Without crevasses to fall into."

Arne pulled off his boots and rubbed his ankle. The trapper did know best, and he was a friend.

"Let's go over your map," Hans said.

For a moment Arne hesitated. I must trust him, he thought.

He took the map from its hiding place and handed it to Hans.

They began to plot the route.

❄ 14 ❄

The blizzard did not let up. It worsened as the day crept on.

Disheartened, Arne fidgeted while Hans calmly went about making bread: punching it down, shaping it into loaves, shoving them into the oven.

"The wind is like a thousand voices, all untrained," Hans said.

But to Arne, the wind was like the long-drawn-out screech of some fearful monster.

It started far away, got louder and louder, closer and closer, hurled itself against the hut, clutching at loose boards—anything in its way. It wound around and around the hut, shaking it until the curtains stood out like sails and the next moment were sucked back onto the windowpane. Tongues of snow, fine as smoke, sharp as needles, came through cracks in the walls.

Then, suddenly, the wind faded, only to begin all over again—again—and again—until Arne pounded on the wall and yelled, "STOP."

"It will," Hans said. "In its own time."

"It will blow the hut away before it stops," Arne cried.

Hans shook his head. "This hut has stood for many winters. Here, ignorance is the killer."

"Ignorance?"

"Of how to survive," Hans said. "It killed a hutful of soldiers just a few months ago, not many miles from this very spot."

"Soldiers?"

"Frozen. All of them. They took refuge in a hut. When the door was opened, they fell out like so many matchsticks."

"Where did they come from?"

"That's not known. Maybe a landing party, maybe from a torpedoed German warship. . . ."

"Germans. GOOD!" Arne spat out.

"NO," Hans shouted, raising a fist.

Arne drew back.

The wind roared down the iron stovepipe, blew the door of the oven open, and clouds of cinders scattered into the room.

"IGNOMINIOUS!" Hans raved. He rushed to the oven, brushed cinders from his browning loaves. "Done," he said, smiling broadly now. "And what do you think we have to go with it? Cloudberry jam."

Cloudberry jam! Arne had not had any since Norway. He devoured half a loaf of the bread and a good part of the jam before he really thought about it. To borrow a hut and find such treats as flour and jam was certainly a surprise.

Other things here were strange.

He hobbled about the hut, examining the books. They were in several languages. In one corner was a row of Bibles, again in different languages.

He ran his hands over the carved bears. He thought they were very good.

An old trunk stood against one wall. Arne tried to lift the lid. Locked.

When he glanced up, the trapper's gaze was on him. For that instant, Hans seemed threatening. A prickle of apprehension ran through Arne. Was Hans really a trapper? He'd test him. "When I was outside, I saw ptarmigan. They would be good with the fresh bread for supper."

"There are lentils here," Hans said. "Lentil soup is also good with fresh bread. Who wants to go out in this unweather to bag ptarmigan?"

Arne could not fault the answer.

That night Arne lay awake in the upper bunk. Questions twirled about in his mind. Why had Hans been so angry at Arne's reaction to the death of the German soldiers? All Norwegians, unless they were quislings, were against the invader.

There was something mysterious about the hut. Hans was very much at home in it, almost as if it were his. Could this be? There were animals skins—bear, deer, walrus—on the walls and on the bunks, but had Hans really bagged them? Hans, who could not shoot a sleeping seal?

Questions, many questions. All unanswered. While Arne

brooded, the savagery of the storm diminished. Did that mean they could leave tomorrow? He'd ask Hans. The lamp was still lit.

He sat up and looked over the edge of his bunk. Hans was close to the stove, doing something with his hands. He was carving a bear.

Arne lay back. His mind did flip-flops. The hut must belong to Hans.

No, not possible. It belonged to an educated man.

Below, he heard the chair scrape against the floor. The light went out. Hans moved in the lower bunk.

Why, Arne wondered, had he not come out and asked Hans directly about the hut?

Deep down, Arne knew the answer. He was afraid.

Of what?

He did not know.

❋ **15** ❋

Arne came awake with a start. Had he dreamed that frightening moan?

He sat up.

The storm?

No, outside it was deadly quiet. The storm was over. Jubilantly, he slid down from his bunk and tested his ankle. Good.

Kara got up from where she lay next to Hans' bed, stretched and came to him.

The moan again. It came from Hans' bunk. A nightmare probably.

Arne turned toward him, shook his shoulder. "The storm is over. We can go," he said.

Hans turned feverish eyes toward him. "I'm freezing. Keep the fire going," he gasped.

Arne heaped wood on the dying embers, put on the kettle.

Hans was shivering. "Arne, malaria back again, medicine in the chest, key on a hook behind the clock."

Arne sprang to the chest and unlocked it.

The lid creaked as he raised it. A murky smell came from the chest's interior. He dug through photographs, books, clothing, to find a box with medicines, which he took to Hans.

"Quinine," Hans said, pointing to a bottle of tablets.

Arne brought a mugful of water to Hans, who was shaking so violently he spilled it.

Arne hurried to find more bedclothes. He made tea, gruel. All the while his mind groped with his problems. His need to reach his father, Hans' sudden sickness.

Hans was quieter now.

Arne gulped breakfast, his map propped up against the medicine box.

He figured seventy more miles to his father. Six days left to reach him. Time was running out. As he folded the map, his glance fell on the box of medicines. It was old, made of some kind of metal. He had not noticed the lid before—an etching of a city, some of it worn off. At the bottom, the name of the city—Hamburg. Hamburg, GERMANY. GERMANY!

Fear shot through him with needle pricks. The box meant nothing, a souvenir box. Now unexplained things jumped into Arne's mind to nag him. The trapper's insistence on helping find Arne's father, the many kindnesses, all of them leading to his father—*after* Hans knew his father was wanted by the Nazis.

Hans was asleep now. Arne stood next to his bed and studied his face. If Hans shaved, what would he look like? Far different. Only the hair on his face made him appear rough, uncouth.

The man was helpless, yet Arne felt unsafe, as if he were teetering on the edge of a crevasse.

Foolish. Hans had been good to him. And yet . . .

Across the room, the lid of the chest still stood open and drew Arne. Quietly he went over to the corner, knelt before the chest, began to go through its contents. A fine suit, black. The label inside the coat—a Hamburg tailor. There were many photographs, family pictures, all with the imprint of a German photographer.

All but one—of a young man in the uniform of a German officer and taken in a desert country. On the back of the photograph in heavy script, he read, "AFRICA, 1917."

Something about the face was familiar. The eyes—deep-set, intense. The young man clean-shaven, but if he had hair on his face . . . HANS!

Softly, Arne closed the chest.

Now he knew.

His legs were weak as he got to his feet.

"Arne, the fever, a little water," Hans begged. "Thank you, thank you, Arne."

Arne put on sweater and anorak and went outside for more wood.

He sawed meat for the dog.

He gave the trapper his medicine. He put food close by. Water.

"Tonight and tomorrow will be the worst," Hans mumbled. "The crisis. We'll reach your father in time. I know shortcuts."

Arne pulled his rucksack over his shoulders.

The trapper watched, eyes wild. He tried to sit up and fell back. "Wait, Arne, wait."

Arne went to the door, looked back.

Hans seemed more dead than alive.

The dog followed Arne outside.

Arne buckled on his skis and pushed off.

He looked back. The dog was following. Well, why not?

The smooth snow was marked with an occasional track.

He saw the mark of a fox. Once he saw the print of a bear. He did not want to meet up with a bear.

Suddenly Arne realized Kara was no longer with him.

He turned.

She was way behind, standing still, her tail lowered.

"Kara!"

She ran to him.

"Let's go."

The dog seemed puzzled.

Arne thrust his poles into the snow and went forward. He looked back. Kara was running the other way.

Arne did not call her again. But as he skimmed over the snow and glided around curving hills, her puzzled look haunted him.

After a time he stopped to check his compass and look at his map.

He was ready to go again when, racing toward him came a herd of reindeer. They halted abruptly some thirty feet from him, their white coats blending with the snow. They turned away.

Before Arne could recover from his surprise, they were

back again. Closer now, watching him. If he were a trapper with a gun, he could pick off whichever one he wanted. Didn't they know that?

Their curiosity satisfied, they walked away lazily.

They trusted him. Didn't they know that was dangerous?

He didn't trust, and because he didn't, he had left a man who might die. If he could not reach his medicine, if he could not keep the fire going, Hans would die. A man who twice had saved his life. Should he have tried to trust Hans in spite of what he had discovered in the chest? He didn't know.

He stood there and he realized how young he was. Twelve years old, and he must make a decision about life and death.

He remembered the disbelief in Hans' eyes when he had left.

Hans had begged for time. "We'll reach your father. I know shortcuts."

In order to give Hans what he asked for, Arne had to trust him.

"I have to go back," Arne said. "I have to go back."

❄ 16 ❄

From far off he saw Kara waiting at the door of the hut. She ran to meet him, wagging her tail furiously. When Arne took off his skis and pushed in the door, the dog squeezed in ahead and ran to Hans' bed.

He was just as Arne had left him.

The fire was almost out.

The gruel was untasted.

Even before taking off his anorak, Arne piled wood onto the embers and took medicine to Hans. He was burning up, throwing off the covers, delirious.

Arne nursed him for two more days, frightened for Hans, frightened for his own father. During the second night the fever broke. Hans was drenched in sweat. Arne brought him warm, dry clothes. They had to be changed again and again.

Toward morning, Arne dozed in a chair beside him. When he awakened, the trapper was trying to sit up. He was rational. His eyes were steady on Arne. "You came back. Why?"

"I don't know. You're a German, a German officer. I saw what was in the chest. The Gestapo is after my father. We can't go home to Norway. I don't know why I came back. Maybe I'm like the reindeer I saw. They came back for a second look at me, to see what I really was, I guess. Maybe I had to do the same."

Hans managed a wan smile. "Whatever the reason, I'm grateful." He sighed. "There was a time I too ran away. Unlike the reindeer, I never went back."

He closed his eyes. Arne wanted him to go on. "Why did you run?"

Hans seemed to come back from some far-off place. "I was a chaplain. For four years I saw the stupidity, the waste of war."

He paused, as if the memories were too painful.

After a moment he went on. "After it was over, I had a church in Hamburg. When the second war was coming, I knew I could not go through it again."

Hans looked spent, but Arne wanted to hear the rest. "How did you get away?"

"As a student I had spent much time in Norway. I knew Spitsbergen. Norwegian ships often came into the port of Hamburg. One day I boarded a freighter. I came here to lead my life alone, without disorder, ugliness. I brought my books, and I made a nest for myself. I would kill only when I had no other food. War would never touch me again."

He smiled. "Then you came. War did touch me." He held out his hand. "Give me a lift. I'm shaky, but I can get up. Tomorrow we will go to your father."

As Arne went about getting ready for their departure, one thing still bothered him. How had Hans known about the evacuation? The radio at Longyearbyen had been silenced. Also those on the British ships. And yet, when Arne had arrived half-dead at Hans' hut, he had known about it.

No, Arne decided, he would not ask.

He believed Hans' story.

He would trust.

✳ 17 ✳

Images—frightening, thrilling, awesome—imprinted themselves on Arne's mind as they sped north. Icebergs, blue-tinged in the wan sunshine. Snow, fine as flour, squeaking beneath skis. A yellow moon present day and night. Air so clear the ends of the earth were visible. A glimpse of musk-oxen, the fresh tracks of hugh bear paws.

Worries. Could Hans keep up the terrific pace? Would he become ill again? How about Kara? Would they reach the great ice wall in time? Or would they find his father had already left and was returning to Longyearbyen and the Nazis?

There was a moment of terror. An ice bear and two cubs

stared across the frozen whiteness at them. Arne was ready to bolt. "Stay," Hans commanded both Arne and Kara.

The mother bear turned tail, the cubs following. "She'd rather eat seal," Hans said, taking his hands from the gun.

Shreds of pale sunshine hung in the clouds and disappeared into blue night. Hans announced, "I know a hotel close by."

"Hotel?"

"An old bear's cave. Abandoned," Hans said. "Safe."

The two-room bear hotel—dry and warm. Hans heating beans on a Primus.

Cozy.

Arne watched the shadows, unable to completely forget the former owner.

And he awoke the next morning, exhilarated, filled with joy. Today was the day he would see his father.

Apprehension.

The hunt for the camp amid sheer walls of ice, domes of crystal, bizarre, unreal shapes.

They were too late.

Had it all been for nothing?

Hans faltering, Kara tired, Arne felt defeat. Cold chilled him to the bone.

Suddenly he saw thin smoke rising. A mirage?

Closer now. A tent, two men, Father's voice. Arne falling into strong arms. Tears freezing on his face. A heavy weight lifted, and Arne was a child again, home with his father.

Hans forgotten, then remembered and pulled into the circle.

Father moved them toward shelter, warmth, food.

The Swiss scientist served up boiling soup.

Thawing, emerging from an ice cocoon. Arne was alive again.

Now Father asked questions. "What has happened? Why are you here?"

Arne told him.

His father was shocked.

"There was no way to let you know that you must not come back to Longyearbyen, that the Nazis were expected to invade," Arne said. "The radio was silenced. The evacuation had to be secret."

Arne's father struggled to control his feelings. "You stayed behind, you came all this distance. . . ."

"Father, I had no choice, not after I saw the first Nazi ship in the harbor. I could not have made it if I had not found Hans' hut. He saved my life."

"And you saved mine," Hans said.

Arne's father covered his face with his hands. Then he grasped Arne's shoulders tightly. "My son," he said, "how you have grown up."

The Swiss passed a steaming platter. "We thought our radio had failed. Tomorrow we would have been on our way to Longyearbyen."

Kara, well fed, lay under the table, content.

The meal finished, the talk turned to escape.

"Arne and I shall take our chances on a passing boat," Arne's father said.

"That is what an old trapper hoped to do," Hans interrupted. "He stopped by my hut just before Arne came. He had come from Longyearbyen, and he told me of the evacuation. He did not want to leave the Arctic. He said he would sit out the war in Iceland. I hope he made it."

Arne, listening, was thankful he had not asked Hans how

69

he had known about the evacuation. He was glad he had trusted.

The Swiss decided to return via Longyearbyen. "The Germans will allow a Swiss to pass, and I shall have Hans' company part of the way."

"I had hoped Hans would come with us," Arne's father said.

Hans shook his head. "Kara and I will stay. But after the war is over, we shall meet again."

They gripped hands with the promise.

Later Arne went outside the tent. Kara snuggled up against him.

Arne dug his fingers into the dog's thick fur. How could he say good-bye? His father came to stand beside him, his arm across Arne's shoulder.

They watched the Northern Lights move against the sky. Often Arne had seen them, but never as they were now, shining extravagantly, greenish to white, the stars and the moon glowing through the transparent veils.

The lights flashed across the sky continuously, as if they were sending a message of hope. The war would end one day. Arne and his father would return to Norway. The world would be right again.

✳ Epilogue ✳

Arne and his father made their escape via a fishing boat to the Shetland Islands and, eventually, to England.

On September 3, 1943, the German superbattleship *Tirpitz,* a cruiser and ten destroyers left the Norwegian fjord where they were hiding and headed for Spitsbergen. Longyearbyen was burned to the ground. The mines were set on fire.

On November 15–16, 1944, a British bomber spied the *Tirpitz* as she hid along an island in the neighborhood of Tromso, Norway, and dropped a bomb. It fell so close in the shallow sea that the battleship tipped over and lay bottom side up.

When the war was over and Norway was finally liberated, Arne and his father returned.

Arne was now seventeen.

They kept their pact to meet with Hans. They came together in Tromso, gateway to Spitsbergen. It was the time of the Midnight Sun, of music and laughter.

It took half the midsummer golden night to catch up on what had happened. . . . Longyearbyen was being rebuilt. There were greetings from Nils, from the Paulsons, warm invitations to Arne and his father to visit.

Later, Father, Arne and Hans got a lift on a small motorboat to the place where the capsized *Tirpitz* stuck out of the water. Together they walked over its flat hull.

"It was all so useless," Father said.

"Ignominious," Hans said.

"Ignominious," Arne echoed.